S0-AEL-394

For Lizbit
–Jen

SLEEPING BEAR PRESS™
2395 South Huron Parkway, Suite 200, Ann Arbor, MI 48104
www.sleepingbearpress.com © Sleeping Bear Press
Printed and bound in the United States
10 9 8 7 6 5 4 3 2 1
Library of Congress Cataloging-in-Publication Data
Names: Sattler, Jennifer Gordon, author, illustrator.
Title: Rock and Vole / written and illustrated by Jennifer Sattler.
Description: Ann Arbor, MI : Sleeping Bear Press, [2021] | Audience:
Ages 4-8. | Summary: "A perfectionist vole gets frustrated when a large
boulder impedes her planned adventure"– Provided by publisher.
Identifiers: LCCN 2021005400 | ISBN 9781534111035 (hardcover)
Subjects: CYAC: Adaptability (Psychology)–Fiction. | Voles–Fiction. | Rocks–Fiction.
Classification: LCC PZ7.S24935 Ro 2021 | DDC [E]–dc23
LC record available at https://lccn.loc.gov/2021005400

ROCK and VOLE

Written and illustrated by Jennifer Sattler

PUBLISHED by SLEEPING BEAR PRESS™

Vole began each day
with some light stretching.

Followed by exactly
7 minutes of exercise.

Each day at snack time she would eat:

1 slice of pumpernickel bread

with 2 pieces of stinky cheese and 12 raisins.

Each day ended the same way—
with a long, comfortable sleep
on the left side of the bed.

But one morning, Vole woke up
wanting something different.
She wanted an adventure.

She started to make a plan. She drew a map.

She picked a spot exactly halfway to stop for her snack of stinky cheese and raisins on pumpernickel.

And at the end of her journey,
she planned to celebrate her adventure and say,
"This is just as I imagined it."

The next morning Vole was on her way.

Soon the sun was high in the sky.
The map showed that she was halfway there—snack time.
After eating, she did some light stretching.

She was right on schedule when . . .

there it was . . .

...a humongous,
GINORMOUS rock.

"Whaat?!
This should NOT be here!
There's no ginormous rock on my map!"

"Look at this map.
Do you see any humongous rocks?!"

The rock was silent. It seemed to be ignoring her.

Vole tried to calm herself.
Surely this rock would
listen to reason.

"Excuse me, Rock,
I've planned this trip
very carefully.

As you can see, you don't belong here. I'm sure you understand."

The rock just sat there.

She tried another way.
"Pretty please, Rock,
could you just do me a teeny-weeny
favor and go sit somewhere else?"

The rock did not move.

Vole was losing her patience. She had not planned on standing out in the hot sun arguing with a giant rock.

She moved closer to the rock where there was some shade.

"That's better. At least you're good for something."

It had been hours since Vole had left home.
She should have been at the end
of her journey by now,
not stuck somewhere in between.

"Stop looking
at me like that.
You ruined
everything."

The rock was silent,
listening.

"See?
I had a perfect plan.
I was going on an
adventure!"

It was afternoon now and the sun
had slid further down in the sky.

The rock looked . . . different.

Vole whispered, “You’re lovely.
Can I take your picture?”

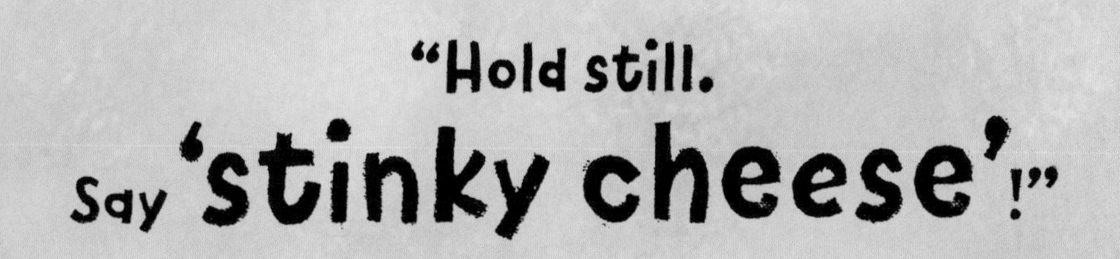
"Hold still.
Say 'stinky cheese'!"

Vole looked at the picture of her and the rock.
The rock glowed in the sunset.
Behind them, the sky was red and purple.

She snuggled up close to the warm rock.

Using her crayons, she made a few changes to her map.

Together they looked
at the sky. Vole sighed.
"This isn't quite
what I imagined," she said.

"It's much, much better."

Gentle breeze
START
Yum!
SNack Time